DEATH IN A DAY

Death is recruiting.

Clayton M. Troke

https://www.deathinaday.com

Print Edition
ISBN10: 0-9793080-9-7
ISBN13: 978-0-9793080-9-3

Published by: Sid Narged Publishing House
http://www.sidnarged.com

This is dedicated to the pursuit of the "panacea."

CONTENTS

Title Page

Copyright

Dedication

Introduction.

The Appointment.   1

The Case.   5

The 'Rona.   9

Dre's House.   13

Down the road to Petersburg.   17

Chance's Chance.   21

Meadowbridge Avenue, Henrico.   25

The Drive... and The Stop.   27

David the Brave.   31

Alley behind Sam's house.   35

David's Apartment on North Avenue.   39

Chance's Apartment on North Avenue.   43

Chet and his coffee.   47

David's Vigil.   51

David and Goliath.   55

Epilogue   59

The Author Biography   61

INTRODUCTION.

RVA Summer, 2020.   In Richmond, Virginia, there are many historic events occurring. These cultural and social changes, as well as the people who initiate that change, deserve recognition.

However...

In the waning days of July, the string of fate has been tugged and dark forces manipulate the futures of the innocent. As a result, some of their stories will end prematurely... and violently.

These souls have been selected to participate in another grand endeavor... death.

What if death isn't just the condition of being devoid of life, but something more tangible?
What if death is a game?
What if we are hunted?
Recruited?
Even initiated into a circle of death.

Are you the giver?
The taker?
The bringer?
Or the maker?

What if today is your day to face Death?

THE APPOINTMENT.

July 10th, 2020 – Early Afternoon.

The scene is a small home office in an affluent Richmond neighborhood – Monument Avenue. A veteran in his late-50's named Chet holds a Video Conference with his Psychologist from nearby McGuire Hospital, to address his complaints about everything. Chet has a good life, but he was encouraged to take early retirement from the police force. He postulates that it was due to vocalizing some less-than-kind opinions about the riots and the people protesting outside his home. Coincidently, he may have been overly aggressive in his crowd-control duties as well.

He complains throughout his allotted time, while his psychologist listens quietly;

- He can't believe they are tearing down the monuments.
- Robert E. Lee is right outside his house.
- His wife is related to Lee.
- His home value is plummeting because of "these people."
- His son is even dating one of "them."
- "They" are always blocking the alley behind his house where his garage is… etc.

This is going to take a while.

Outside is a gathering of people at the Robert E. Lee monument, covered in graffiti. It is as he said… "they" are blocking his alley, and his garage. But the protesters are not the only ones around – for death lurks near, and there is nothing that anyone can do about it.

A tall, bald, chocolate-skinned male approaches the end of the alley and pauses for a moment. He is well-dressed, well-groomed, and stands tall. The only inkling that he may not be a banker or a doctor is his red "I can't breathe!" mask and large tattoo of a scythe on the side of his head. It is hot and he is sweating, but he doesn't appear to be otherwise affected. He removes the mask, coughs into it once, wipes his head with it, and drops it on the ground. A slight grin crosses his lips as he turns away from the alley and continues up North Allen avenue, away from the protest.

As his time winds down, the doctor tells Chet to do some diaphragmatic breathing and some mindfulness exercises, to which Chet reminds them that he was a sniper and knows all about controlling his breathing.

Chet's son, Sam, is behind the house with his girlfriend, Shauna, and their mutual friend Chance. Shauna met Sam at VCU in Dr. Ok's Black Political Thought class. She found Sam to be pretty authentic and endearing for a spoiled, rich, white kid. Chance, on the other hand, has always been looking for his chance with Shauna, or any other girl they run into. While he is not her favorite person, they have spent enough time together that they get along.

The trio are on an extended summer break from VCU, as last semester was a wash due to the COVID-19 restrictions. Henceforth, they have had some extra time in their schedules to join in some protests, smoke some pot, and basically concern themselves with everything that motivates politically-minded college students.

As the joint shrinks to a roach, and Chet's appointment is lingering, they decide to head toward the rally. On the way, Shauna spots a red mask on the ground and picks it up. She throws it into the air toward the dumpster. Without knowing, she overshoots, and it floats down in the back of Sam's white Jeep. She grabs Sam's hand and laughs as they march into the crowd.

THE CASE.

July 20th, 2020 – Mid Afternoon.

Shauna's younger brother, Diandre, is the sibling closest to her – and not just in age. They have the same father, who was never really "with" their mother – and hasn't been in their lives since Diandre was about two years old. This only strengthens the bond between her and "Dre" (as she affectionately calls him.) He gets into trouble, and hangs with the wrong crew sometimes, but he's her brother – and they are family.

Dre has found himself with his friends Quincy and J.T., loitering in the parking lot of the Food Lion on Forest Hill. Without much going on, J.T. starts fantasizing about scoring some 'Superglue,' but they sadly blew most of their money over the weekend. Dre and Quincy are the followers in this trio. J.T. frequently chides Dre that his sister, Shauna, is more of a man than he is… while Quincy just hopes that J.T. continues to focus his aggression on Dre. As they prepare to abandon their search, Quincy observes a well-dressed man depositing a metal suitcase behind the dumpster. The man promptly slides back into a dark Mercedes G-Wagon and cruises away. This is a bit too curious for the trio, and sensing an opportunity, they collect the bag.

After a brief examination of its contents in the trunk of J.T.'s Honda Civic, they are delighted to discover that they may have hit the jackpot. Loose in the case is a very used, semi-automatic pistol. Dre has never had a gun and isn't sure he wants one. His sister would certainly kick his ass if she found out, and if *she* didn't… *his mother* sure-as-hell would. J.T. already has a Glock and is uninterested in this beat-up old piece. With no other takers, Quincy proudly steps up and claims it. The real score is a strange, cigar box containing a roll of cash and a couple of fist-sized bags of white powder. They divide the cash, but not being very sophisticated in the drug trade, they have no way of assessing the value of the powder in the bags. However, J.T. has a connection who will meet them at the McDonald's across the street and do an "analysis" for them. They clean out the case and dump it back where they found it.

At the allotted time, J.T. leads the crew over. They leave one of the bags in the trunk, just in case. The contact arrives in a Mercedes E-class Sedan and J.T. squeezes into the back. Dre and Quincy, presently rich with cash, go into McDonald's for some food. As they come out, something is wrong – and it's obviously very wrong.

J.T. is backing away from the car and all four of the occupants are now outside. They are threatening him and demanding they turn over the case when Dre and Quincy arrive at his side. In the heat of the moment, Quincy pulls out his newly acquired pistol and fires at the foursome. This is surprisingly effective, striking two of them with each of his first two shots. J.T. is bolstered by this and pulls his Glock. With no weapon, Dre takes off in the direction of the Food Lion. J.T. hits a third by burning through his clip and then bolts. As Quincy tags the last assailant, he himself takes a hit in the side. The three make it to the curb together when Quincy hands Dre the gun and collapses, losing consciousness.

J.T. drags Dre into motion. Witnesses see two armed men running back toward the Food Lion parking lot. J.T. drops Dre back at his home at Chesterfield Village Apartments and tells him to lay low for a couple of days.

Dre conceals the pistol, walks past Shauna, and goes to the bathroom to wash off the blood.

THE 'RONA.

July 22nd, 2020 – Afternoon.

Sam is worried. He's definitely feeling sick. His father, Chet, is already paranoid and tells him to go get tested for COVID. Chet espouses the belief that Sam probably got it from his girlfriend or from hanging out at those rallies that are ruining his home's value and defacing history. Sam texts Shauna; she tells him to get tested. She doesn't want to get her mom or Dre sick, so she won't go with him. Sam is a healthy guy in his 20's and will likely not be killed by the virus. Still, he wants to know if he has it – and so does his father.

Sam dutifully heads to the Henrico Doctors Hospital and gets his quick test. With a swab up his nose, he quips that he could have just picked them a few boogers and saved them the trouble. Even with this being the 5th time the nurse has heard that line today, she still manages a chuckle. However, his nervous humor fades as she returns with the results; he is positive for COVID-19 and is contagious. He should isolate himself and get a list together of anyone he's had close contact with, so they can get tested as well.

He first calls his father and requests permission to come back to the house. He has never faced this situation before and is scared that he will be unwelcome at home. Chet is not going to turn his back on his son, even if he is a "pansy, liberal fuck." He can come home, but his girlfriend is not invited. Sam informs his father that she doesn't want to get her family sick and probably won't see him until he is better anyway.

He sends a quick text to Chance, who replies that he'll "take good care of Shauna" while he's sick.

On his ride back home, he calls Shauna. She immediately regrets telling him that she didn't want to go with him to get tested. Maybe she could have gone, but now that Chet is involved, she won't be allowed over. As they hang up, Shauna gets annoyed that Sam always follows his parents' demands so rigidly. She feels a little heated, perhaps even feverish, as a text from Chance arrives on her phone asking if she wants to "go do anything tonight."

DRE'S HOUSE.

J.T. has been gathering some information about selling "the score." He was put in contact with some guys in Petersburg and they want to meet near the Peabody Middle School at about 2:00 A.M. His Honda Civic pulls in to the Chesterfield Villages lot to pick up Dre. They 'smoke one up' in the parking lot, leaning against the car, and talking about Quincy. They can't believe he's gone. It all happened so fast. They muse for a bit that he turned out to be a pretty good shot and without him, they may have all been killed.

As they prepare to get back into the car, another vehicle creeps slowly past the clubhouse and three younger guys spring out. One is apparently related to the guy that J.T. shot at McDonald's. It immediately erupts into chaos when someone brandishes a gun and starts shooting wildly. Dre dives into the Civic. J.T. pulls out a Glock, fires the entire clip into their car, and bounds into the driver's seat. With flawless muscle memory, he grabs the key, shoves it in the ignition, and speeds off. They cut across Midlothian Turnpike, hop onto Chippenham Parkway, and head toward Petersburg. The other vehicle limps into the WAWA on the corner, where they are later arrested.

All of the neighbors hear the shots, including Shauna. She immediately texts her brother to find out if he's alright. After a few messages saying that he's ok, he stops replying to her inquiries.

Shauna knows that Sam is in lockdown, but she wants to go looking for Dre… so she decides to take her chances with Chance.

DOWN THE ROAD TO PETERSBURG.

Dre is in no mood for his sister to be continually blowing up his phone, so he puts the slider into silent mode. After driving at top speed for a bit and assessing their physical safety, the adrenaline starts to wear off. The car has taken a couple of bullets, but the glass seems to be intact. Neither Dre nor J.T. have been injured and they start dissing their assailants' ineptitude out of nervous bravado. They drive most of the way in silence to regroup their thoughts and reload J.T.'s Glock. They wonder if they should even try to deal with these people or if they should just abandon the stuff somewhere.

As they approach the turn onto Wesley street to meet their connection, they pass a G-wagon Mercedes heading in the opposite direction.

When meeting new contacts, people can be jittery. Since Dre and J.T. have been in two gunfights in the past few days (one being within the last hour), they are BOTH extremely jittery. Nervous people make other people nervous. This interaction almost immediately degrades. These guys know about the case… and they want it all… NOW. Having seen this movie already, J.T. decides to be proactive.

J.T. has a notoriously quick trigger – Fast, but with poor aim – more of a point-and-spray shooter. This time he is double-wielding, a gun in each hand; the second he's purchased with his cut of the money from the case. The mayhem results in a great deal of broken glass and tumult, but only one goon has been grazed in the leg. Dre, who is still back near the car, pulls Quincy's gun, fires two rounds and hits two guys square on. As they speed away, he tags one more. This doesn't stop the injured shooters from blasting out all of the rear glass of the Civic. Dre is rattled having never shot anyone before.

Panic sets in instantly. As they turn back toward I-95, they can see the police lights heading in the direction of their meeting… "That was close." Their vehicle is an obvious cop magnet now, shot out glass and riddled with holes. J.T. gets the idea of heading toward his friend's party pad near the raceway. He lives in an old insurance office, across from a crappy little car lot. Perhaps they can boost a car and dump the Civic down the street in front of the towing place. The parties run all night… maybe they'll have some ideas.

Dre and J.T. continue in silence, listening only to the sound of the wind and Waze keeping a constant vigil for police up ahead.

CHANCE'S CHANCE.

Chance immediately jumps at the opportunity to offer Shauna any assistance. He picks her up and they start driving around aimlessly. He rarely gets her alone and she really seems to be rattled. Her throat sounds dry like she's been yelling, but her voice has always been a little raspy. She starts unloading the story of the shooting and her brother, in addition to all of the other violence and recent injustices. She complains of Sam's dad being a crooked, racist cop, who assaulted some of the protesters back in June. After ranting for a while, she gets herself worked into a coughing fit and asks to stop for a drink… Chance suggests that it should be a stiff one.

His apartment on North Avenue is always stocked and ready for this eventuality. To bolster her confidence in him, he asks the cursory questions that mimic the appearance of a person who cares. While filling her drink, he adds a benzo or three to help her "relax." He recently switched from rufies to benzos because they don't have the tattle-tale, blue dye…

"How untrusting the pharmaceutical companies are!"

She quietly sips her drink on the couch trying to figure out where Dre could be. She is frankly amazed at how effective the cocktail is at calming her nerves. After a few minutes of Chance telling her that "there isn't any way to find him," she begins to go blank.

"Don't worry... He's fine."

She had texted him and received a reply that he was ok... Maybe his phone died or he had to save his battery.

"Everything is fine... just relax."

Chance soothes her with empathy and security, as his presence starts to fade into the ether. His voice gradually becomes whispers in her ear and she gently collapses into the crook of his neck. He catches her drink and slowly slips off her shirt.

"Everything is so fine..." crosses his lips as he holds the power button on her phone and shuts it off.

MEADOWBRIDGE AVENUE, HENRICO.

July 23rd, 2020 – 3:00 A.M.

J.T. and Dre dump the Civic in front of the Great Deal Tow Yard on the grass by the street. They leave the keys in the ignition, hoping that someone will steal it - literally driving suspicion away from them. They walk down the street and turn onto Savannah, where J.T.'s friends are obviously involved in a binge. The music is loud, the people are louder, and there seems to be an air of unrest – something about a delivery being late. These parties have become regular around here. Dre is beginning to get nervous. He's the youngest one, and while J.T. is a little older, it's obvious that he isn't the "Alpha dog" either. J.T. is acting uncharacteristically reserved in this situation; he's in over his head and could use some help. This appears as a weakness to the older members of the group who berate both of them and tell them to "grow a pair."

J.T. is not used to being the target of abuse - he is usually the source. He begins to put his balls back on, but it's too late. The elders have no urge to listen to his "pussy flapping" and he can go "suck his bitch's dick." Dre can see that diplomacy has failed them. He concludes that they should go get another car, or get back to the Civic to devise another plan. Being verbally cornered and attacked has unfortunately triggered J.T.'s fight-or-flight response – it has all been too much… too fast. Driven to the point of cracking, he reacts out of blind rage. In doing so, he makes one fatal miscalculation – he hasn't reloaded. He pulls out both Glocks, but each one fires only a single round before the slides lock back. Amazingly, he hit someone with each round. Regrettably, neither was the person who was directly in front of him.

Dre draws his pistol in just enough time to watch J.T. get 3 rounds fired into him at close range. Dre returns a single round taking down the attacker. Pursued, he sprints around the corner, jumps back in the Civic, and drives off. With no idea what to do, he decides it would be a good time to find his sister. She always seems to know what to do. He texts her, but gets no reply. Perhaps she went to Sam's place to unwind? He decides that's the most likely scenario and turns toward Monument Avenue – alone.

THE DRIVE... AND THE STOP.

Cutting across town from the Raceway to Monument is a fairly simple endeavor, but the car Dre is driving is a rolling violation; it has most of the glass shot out and bullet holes everywhere. He needs to get somewhere he can feel safe and unload his mind. He decides it would be prudent to stay off the main roads, so he turns into a residential neighborhood. Dre begins replaying the various situations over and over in his mind - marveling at how effectively he was able to land each of his shots.

Dre starts running an inventory.

- Quincy shot 3 guys with three bullets, right?
- There were the guys in Petersburg... 3 more...
- One for J.T....

This choked him up a little.

7 rounds total. How many bullets does this thing hold? He's not going to check now. He hates to admit that he doesn't know much about guns. It has a safety, a magazine, bullets and a trig-

ger...

...and every time this particular trigger has been pulled... someone gets hit. While this is a somewhat comforting thought, it's also a morbid one. Does it always hit its target? What is this old gun?

The whistling of the wind is getting to him; he muses that not having glass makes the car loud.

He ponders this for only a second before decelerating as he approaches a nightmare situation - a traffic stop. Because he has been avoiding the main roads, he now finds himself on a narrow street with nowhere to turn around. There isn't a lot of time to assess the situation. The cop appears to be in his cruiser and the driver of the other vehicle is likely still in his. Maybe he's broken down? Dre slows to a crawl. Should he pass? He instinctively grabs the gun off the passenger seat.

"Do it..."

DAVID THE BRAVE.

July 23rd, 2020 – 3:15 A.M.

David has been having a tough year. With the COVID-19 pandemic closing down his company, he has been relying on friends to find him odd jobs. Tonight, he is supposed to be delivering a "package" of unknown contents to some old insurance place by the raceway – but it isn't going well. He turned down a side street off of Laburnum when he noticed a police car tailing him. He wasn't speeding and has no criminal record, but this isn't a bundle of roses he's carrying. David delivers to this place frequently, and the guys are always having a party. He knows that it's a small package in a Kroger bag - and it's worth 50 bucks to him.

The lights come on behind him and he pulls to the side. It's a narrow road and while there isn't a lot of room, it's better to stay off of the grass so they don't think he's been drinking. The cop pulls in behind him and David gathers up his license and registration. He starts having some pretty mundane, but seemingly important, questions run through his mind.

What are the appropriate protocols to follow when facing this predicament during the current COVID-19 pandemic?

- Should you take off your mask for the traffic stop or leave it

> on? Maybe you should pull it down over your chin?
> - Do they even take your license and registration?
> - Should you just crack the window?
> - Aren't they only pulling people over for serious issues?
> - How are they doing breathalyzers? Are they sterilized? Have they ever been sterilized? (Gross!!!)

David has always used these lines of mundane and unrelated questions to occupy his mind in stressful situations. It keeps him from dwelling on the relevant and stressful questions that would make him panic. You could say that this is how he maintains his "game face."

He sees the policeman's door open behind him and, as he prepares to roll down his window, he hears a loud "pop!" Looking in the mirror, it appears that a car tried to pull around and maybe he hit the cop's door or something.

> - Did he hit the cop car?
> - Is he drunk or something?
> - Is the cop going to just let him go?
> - Is the other guy going to take the heat off him so he can make this delivery?

While he's pondering this, the car pulls around carefully and slowly creeps by him. David looks up to catch a glimpse of a grinning black man in a very damaged Honda Civic continuing down the street. While he thinks that it's odd, he's just a bit more concerned about his own circumstances right now. He wants to get out of this situation and move on with his life.

Speaking of which, isn't this taking a long time?

He has lost sight of the cop in his mirrors. The lights are blinding him. He can see that the cruiser's door is still open. Maybe he was indeed tail-ended and is checking for damage. That guy must be pretty bold; to smash into a cop car, and just drive off - smiling like that.

What is taking so long?

Is that something on the ground back there?

ALLEY BEHIND
SAM'S HOUSE.

Dre has been to Sam's house a couple of times and knows about the back alley where people park their cars. Sam's Jeep is perched next to their garage. Maybe his sister is spending the night after the shooting earlier. They always "sneak" her up the spiral fire-escape to Sam's room, so she doesn't have to put up with Chet. Chet knows that they do this, as the stairs go right past his bedroom, but he doesn't want to deal with her either. He disapproves of their relationship, but he is permissive. His wife likes Shauna and she is always respectful to him, but he privately hopes that this is a phase that Sam will grow out of.

Dre tries texting Shauna once more before trying Sam... Nothing.

He texts Sam and asks if he can talk to Shauna. He goes on to say that his sister is ignoring his texts, he is worried, and needs to find her. With deft fingers, he slings out one last message informing Sam that he's just out back in the alley.

Sam knows how much these two rely on each other. He puts on a mask and heads down the fire escape to talk to him. Dre looks bad. Sam tells him that he hasn't spoken with Shauna since yesterday afternoon. Dre recounts the shooting at his house as the last time he heard from her. He shrewdly omits any of the rest of the details of the evening since then. Sam tries calling her and the phone instantly goes to voicemail – he hangs up.

Strange. If she were home, the phone would be on and charging. She never shuts off her phone. Now… Sam is getting worried. He concludes that Dre should call his mom and ask if she's home. They still have a land line, but it's practically a direct line to their mother. Dre cringes before pressing the send button.

For a fifty-three second phone call, it was quite informative.

- Don't ever call this fucking late.
- She is going to fucking kill him when he gets home.
- Shauna texted him 100,000 fucking times.
- That fucking Ain't-got-no-Chance kid picked her up hours ago and she guesses that they went to Sam's.

To evade further wrath by worrying his mother, he strategically glosses over the fact that she hasn't been to Sam's and hangs up. Sam's face drops under his mask when he gets this news and he decides to text Chance.

Nothing… and the phone call goes directly to voicemail.

"Damnit."

Sam is a good guy, a bit of a wussy, but his sister could do worse. Dre worries that he may have inadvertently exposed an awkward situation. Sam runs back upstairs to get some real clothes and keys. This wakes up his dad, who has sleep issues due to his military trauma and police service. Dre doesn't care for Sam's dad at all. He can hear Chet giving an extended dissertation about how "that girl" wasn't supposed to be coming over, because she gave him "this shit." Chet continues his rant, "Those people caused this. Why can't you just forget about all this useless hippy shit."

Dre's blood begins to boil, but he can hear Sam defending Shauna and telling Chet that he's just going over to Chance's house…

"So… chill out," he concludes.

Sam comes down the escape and pops out where his Jeep is parked. There is a haze of light beginning to cross the horizon. Sam's anxiety has escalated. He's hoping that Shauna just needed to get out of the house. Perhaps she didn't feel safe or she's out looking for Dre. The pair get in the Jeep. Dre grabs the red "I can't Breathe!" mask off the floor and puts it on. As they leave, Sam nearly backs into an unknown Honda Civic and quizzically asks how Dre got there…

"Uber."

EXTRA
Nº408

DAVID'S APARTMENT ON NORTH AVENUE.

Dave is freaking out. He parked his car in the back alley to keep it out of sight. He still has the package and he's pacing incessantly. His mind won't stop. Is there anywhere he can go? What is happening!?!?

He needs to slow down and focus on the facts. He begins to re-play the events in his mind.

He was pulled over. He sat in his car for what seemed like forever. He didn't want to get out, because he was unsure of the proper protocol. Eventually, he got out of his own car and started looking around. It didn't take him long to discover what had happened. The officer's body was crumpled on the ground, his eyes locked open, and blood pooling around his head. David bolted back to his car and sped off.

His automatic response was to finish his delivery. It was only a couple minutes away, and then he could get rid of the package. As he approached the drop, he could see more flashing lights. The area was loaded with cops! There were police blocking the street and putting up tape. Was that another body!?!?!? Oh man.

Dave comes back to his senses. He's safe at home now… sort of.

- What is he going to do?
- Did they run his plate?
- Do they have his address?
- Do they even know about the other cop?
- Are they going assume that he shot the cop?
- Are they going to then conclude that he had something to do with the other shooting too?!?!?
- Did the guy in that Civic shoot him?

Dave's modus operandi of asking mundane and unrelated questions seems to be failing him at this moment.

He decides that he should tell his friend about the delivery first. He rambles on about the cops, and how he thinks something went down before he got there. He still has possession of the package and can return it, but his friend isn't happy with this turn of events. This delivery would have been worth a lot of money to him. The guy who set this up isn't going to be happy. His friend tells him to give him a few minutes and he'll call him back.

He starts pacing around wondering if he was somehow responsible for the incident. As if completing the delivery would have stopped the shooting from happening somehow. What's in this bag anyway? Dave is now curious as to exactly what this package contains. He has never been explicitly told that he shouldn't look inside, only to deliver it.

Was it even implied that he shouldn't look? Maybe he just made that assumption? This line of thinking leads him to the conclusion that he should look in the bag.

He gently unties the knot, trying his best to keep it intact, and peeks inside. He sees a strange small box with a weird skeleton on it. Inside that is a roll of cash and a bag of white powder. The box is strangely intriguing to him. The art is like nothing he has ever seen. There is a fabric lining in the box, and inscribed on the trim are the words "Romeo y Julieta."

What a strange box.

His cell phone vibrates... startling him. It's his friend. He informs David that someone is coming to drop off a case in about an hour. He is instructed to put the package in the case, take it behind the old Dry-Tac building off Charles City road near the airport, and drop it next to the porta-john. David just needs to be outside his apartment at 5:15 - They'll be there.

CHANCE'S APARTMENT ON NORTH AVENUE.

Chance is getting frustrated. This has never happened before. He's tried everything, but Shauna has stopped breathing. He's dumped water on her, slapped her, put her in the shower, tried CPR… everything he could think of… but nothing. She's gone. Normally, if he were in a really bad situation, his first call would be to Sam. He can't bring himself to make that call this time, however. He's shut off her phone and no one knows that she's there… he should be fine. He just needs to get rid of her. He starts Googling murderers and body disposal methods, best places to drop a corpse, etc. This isn't really his bag, but neither is jail. He decides that he doesn't have the stomach to cut her up. Maybe he should just roll her up in blankets and dump her somewhere far away.

"Road Trip!" He chuckles to himself. He's already got her clothes off. He can donate those to Goodwill or something. Any clothing drop will do… spread it out in time and distance. No rush. Her body is still in the bathroom. He takes great care and cleans her well to remove any evidence, then lays out a blanket to wrap her up.

He takes his time, posing her on the floor. He stares at her for a second…

Was that a knock? No. It can't be. It's almost 5:00 in the morning.

*Knock*Knock*Knock*

Sam's voice is muffled, but he recognizes it immediately. He's talking to someone. Think fast. He throws all her clothes in the bathroom and quickly turns on the shower, locks the door, and closes it behind him. Chance composes himself and works over the story quickly in his head…

- She texted him after the shooting. = True.
- He went to get her. = True.
- She was frustrated with Sam. = True.
- She was freaking out because of the shooting and finding Dre. = True.
- They had a couple drinks. = True.
- She took some pills. = Technically True.
- He had sex with her. = Sam will be pissed, but it's also True.
- She went into the bathroom wrapped in the covers. = Not on her own… but True.
- The shower is running and she's been in there ever since. = True.

He's got this. Breathe… This is going to suck, but even if it comes down to the police, there is reasonable doubt. He doesn't want to lose a friend, but maybe he can salvage this by pinning it on her. Why would she want his help anyway? How is he supposed to know where Dre would go after a shooting in front of his own house? Maybe Dre was the one who did the shooting!?! He could be anywhere by now!

Chance pulls himself together, puts on his "tired face," and opens the door.

Now he knows exactly where Dre is…

CHET AND HIS COFFEE.

Chet is alone with his coffee… fuming.

"At least he won't be giving that shit to us." He mutters.

He flips on his scanner and plops down in front of his laptop. Chet is a news junkie. As a former cop, he likes being on the cutting edge of information. The chatter is lively this morning… which is never good. There was an officer shot making a traffic stop and they are looking for the driver for questioning. A damaged Honda Civic was also recorded by the dash cam at the scene of the crime. This Civic may also be connected to a nearby shooting with 3 injuries and one fatality. Another district is reporting a shooting in Petersburg with 4 more people injured.

"Damn. The world's gone crazy."

He continues to scroll through the news. He reads that Governor Northam is going to have a virtual signing of something called the CROWN ACT, which stands for "Creating a Respectful and Open World for Natural Hair", and is supposed to bring attention to the people who "dismiss and diminish people for no good reasons."

"You can't fucking spell… Get a haircut."

Chet runs his hand across his balding, buzz cut and sips his coffee. He wonders if this bill would also protect unnatural hair – like when Chance fashioned his hair into a purple-peacock-thing? If Sam ever came home looking like that, Chet would personally shave his head… after a good ass-kicking, of course.

Chet chuckles into his coffee - but the nostalgia has got him thinking, "Why did Sam rush over to Chance's place?"

He had heard someone else talking, but couldn't make out who it was.

His coffee needs a refresh. He stands up and walks toward the window. Maybe Sam came back in while he was taking a piss. He doesn't see the Jeep, but he does see a Honda Civic in the back alley that looks like it's been in a firefight.

"Shit."

Chet grabs his gun and keys, then rushes downstairs.

℞ Antikamnia ʒij

DAVID'S VIGIL.

He's nervous, but optimistic. This is almost over. All he needs to do is stay calm. He is proud of how skillfully he reconstructed the knot on the Kroger bag. The connection will be here in just a few minutes and David has been obsessively peering through a gap in the curtains in anticipation of their arrival.

There is a white Jeep parked on the other side of the street. He saw the occupants go into a nearby apartment a little while ago. The driver was a white kid who was wearing a plain, white, N95-style mask. The passenger was a black guy wearing a red mask with something written on it - but he was too far away to read it.

"Just stay calm and keep your eyes open. "

After a couple of minutes, a silver BMW pulls up and parks on the street right in front of his apartment. An older white male with a buzz cut gets out. The man appears agitated and a possibly lost. He's pivoting around like he doesn't know exactly where he's going, but he's mainly focusing on the opposite side of the street where the Jeep is parked.

Chet has only been to Chance's apartment once. Unfortunately, he doesn't know exactly which apartment it is because they had been waiting out by the street when he picked them up. It could be any of the places around here. He has found the Jeep though. That's good… His son wasn't lying to him.

Behind him a door opens and a timid looking young man exits and nods a greeting at Chet. It's difficult to determine his age, or much else for that matter. He's wearing a cloth mask, has dark olive skin, and appears to be in his 20's. He's carrying a Kroger bag and is tentatively approaching; he gently asks if Chet is lost.

Chet doesn't like to admit when he's lost, but he certainly is. His inner police officer takes the most direct tact and asks if he knows the location of the driver of the white Jeep. The young man, who had been walking toward him, stops. He points at the apartment directly across the street and indicates that the driver entered there just a little while ago.

Chet thanks him and begins crossing the road toward the apartment the young man indicated.

David was really hoping that was his connection. He turns to observe a dark Mercedes G-Wagon slowly crawling into his driveway.

POP

Chet freezes in the middle of the street and grabs for his hip. He doesn't see a gun or a shooter, but that certainly sounded like a shot.

The Mercedes pulls up next to David and stops… it's 5:15 on the dot.

DAVID AND GOLIATH.

A man exits the Mercedes, extracting a small, metal case from the passenger seat in one smooth motion. He is a tall, good-looking, bald, black man. The tension is palpable. David is fidgety but the bald man appears calm and unaffected. He straightens his tie, pauses, then silently lifts a single finger into the air – as if he's checking the direction of the wind. He breaks eye contact with David and turns his head to observe the situation unfolding across the street. David takes note of a large scythe tattoo on the side of the man's head, before turning to look as well.

The Jeep's red-masked passenger exists the doorway without hesitation, openly carrying a firearm in his right hand. There is something about the look in his eyes that seems... dead. He is marching straight toward the street. Another person is yelling expletives from inside the now open apartment door. David can only assume that it's either the driver, or the tenant... or both. Buzzcut man is drawing a pistol from his belt and sternly commanding the man to drop his weapon.

Was he a cop?!?
Damnit.

Mr. Red Mask unflinchingly raises his pistol and fires a single shot... the driver of the Jeep simultaneously exits the apartment in a frenzy.

Buzzcut-cop-guy takes the bullet square in the chest, but his own pistol fires before he tumbles to the pavement. His stray round hits the frenzied white kid, who now also collapses. The man with the red mask is still relentlessly striding toward the tattooed man and is now close enough for David to read "I can't breathe!" embroidered in block letters across the mask.

With all of the chaos, David feels strangely calm. He saw the dead cop earlier and has just witnessed two more people get shot right in front of him. He glances over at the tattooed man, who dexterously opens the case and presents it to the gunman like he has just won the contents. The gunman walks coldly past the body in the street, straight up to the man with the case, and removes his mask. David instantly recognizes him as the man from the Civic. The gunman mechanically holds out the pistol and "mic-drops" it into the case. He quickly glances at David, smirks, and turns back toward the Jeep.

David is confused. What is going on? Who are these people? Why doesn't any of this seem to bother him?

The tattooed man now turns toward David with the case still open. David takes a step forward and realizes that it is completely empty, except for the recently-added, beat-up pistol. He gazes back toward the shooter as he starts the Jeep, puts on his mask, and drives away.

The man with the tattoo gently bows his head toward the case. David comprehends this to mean, "Please, place the Kroger bag next to the gun." This somehow appears to be the appropriate action. The man closes the case and quickly spins it around in an expertly choreographed motion. Now holding it by the handle, he extends it robotically toward David, who accepts it.

As the distant sirens intensify, the tattooed man cocks his head to the sky and slides back into the Mercedes.

David starts to panic. The police are almost here and he's holding a bag that is full of drugs, money, and the gun that was used to shoot the man that's lying on the ground in front of him.

What is he going to do?!?!

Seeking guidance, David looks to the man with the tattoo - whose door is still open and doesn't appear to be concerned. His cold stare breaks into a coy smile. For the first time, David hears the voice of death – an icy-smooth sound that runs chills through his entire being.

Just two words slither past his lips...

"Get in."

FRED. SMITH & Cº
Manf'g Chemists
MOTTO
"Quantity not Quality"
NO
GENUINE
GOODS,
SUBSTITUTES
ONLY.

EPILOGUE

July, 1888 – St. Louis, MO. Frank Ruf is struggling with his partner to make their new pharmacy financially viable. Frank has decided to branch out after toiling away as a drug clerk at W.M Alexander's for almost 15 years. His partner Louis Frost is a good drug clerk but a poor businessman. Frank is doing everything he can just to keep it afloat.

While conversing with his friend Dr. Crusius about some new German pharmacological advancements, Crusius recommends that Frank consult with an "old Civil War medic" named Dr. Washington. He was embedded with a detachment of the 62nd US Regiment of Colored Infantry and is well known for his pioneering use of opiate compounds for pain management and war surgery. Crusius adds that he is spoken of highly by Colonel Eli Lilly in Indianapolis, stating that Washington compelled him to start his pharmaceutical company.

Crusius arranges a meeting between Dr. Washington and Frank at the Frost & Ruf Pharmacy to discuss a possible compounding contract. Frank waits anxiously for the designated time as a luxurious carriage pulls up to the front door of their establishment. Inside is a well-dressed, black man that appears far too young to have been an "old Civil War medic." He is skeptical that a black man could even be a military doctor, but Frank is desperate and asks if he is indeed Doctor Washington.

The man exits his carriage with a leather medical bag and immediately unleashes a short monologue in an ice-cold voice.

"Pain is the only thing that people really fear. I have seen many men gratefully welcome death to relieve themselves of their agony. As there is no greater fear, there is also no greater opportunity. Are you interested in the panacea for all suffering?"

Dumbstruck… Frank is initially speechless and can only barely manage to blink. There is something overwhelming about this man – a formidable and dangerous presence. All of the doubts that he was experiencing drain from his mind. His thoughts have become infected with the Greek phrase, "anti-kamnia," meaning "opposed to pain." The words escape his lips, as if the only way to expunge them from his psyche, is to hear them spoken into the world.

The doctor smirks quietly and glances up at the sky, squinting as if he sees something that is not there. He lowers his eyes to the bag, pauses for a second, and hands it over to Frank.

Unable to contain his enthusiasm, Frank immediately opens it and does a quick, visual inventory. Contained within, are some documents, several pharmaceutical tins, and a large bundle of cash.

"What is all this?" Frank asks.

Dr. Washington steps to the side, creating an unobstructed path to the carriage. He motions for Frank to enter with a gentle bow, a wave of his hand, and that smooth, dark voice…

"This is your future, Mr. Ruf…"

"Get in."

THE AUTHOR BIOGRAPHY

(that wasn't.)

Clayton M. Troke is an enigma.

Late July, 2020. I received an email from Clayton; he was inquiring about publishing a short story. When I asked what kind of story it was, he responded simply…

"It's mine."

We exchanged some cursory information about word count and art requirements, but he only seemed interested in getting me to format it and publish it.

He insisted, "…it's already done."

I signed a Non-Disclosure Agreement for him and asked for a manuscript. He immediately sent me a cryptic email about "preparing myself for it." A couple of days later, I received another email with a link to a manuscript, art files, and layout instructions.

I wanted to set up a Zoom meeting so I could get some clarification.

Mr. Troke thusly informed me that he doesn't "do Zoom," and if

I didn't want to publish it, he could take it somewhere else. Ultimately, I made my decision based on a puzzling response he gave to a question I asked...

"What genre should it be classified as?"

To which he responded,

"The tale is fiction... just as life is an ever-evolving fiction. This moment has ended, the torch has been passed, and this chapter is closed... Just publish it."

The final enigma occurred while doing the layout. I asked for a bio and a photo to include in the back matter of the book.

In response, he sent me one photo, and a single sentence...

"This person does not exist."

I convinced him to let me convey this story in its place.

SID NARGED.
PUBLISHER

Death is recruiting.

CLAYTON M. TROKE

For more information visit the Website:
https://www.deathinaday.com

Print Book Information
ISBN 10: 0-9793080-9-7
ISBN 13: 978-0-9793080-9-3